The Best SUKKOT PUMPKIN EVER

This **PJ BOOK** belongs to

_____

_____

To Lyvia, who gifted me a library of picture books that fueled my childhood curiosity. —L.S.

To Gabe and BTBJ preschool, love Pumpkin Head —C.M.

KAR-BEN PUBLISHING
A division of Lerner Publishing Group, Inc.
241 First Avenue North
Minneapolis, MN 55401 USA
1-800-4-KARBEN

Website address: www.karben.com

Main body text set in HandySans Book 16/18.
Typeface provided by MADType.

Library of Congress Cataloging-in-Publication Data

Names: Steinberg, Laya, author. | Madden, Colleen M., illustrator.
Title: The best Sukkot pumpkin ever / by Laya Steinberg ; illustrated by Colleen Madden.
Description: Minneapolis : Kar-Ben Publishing, [2017] | Age 3-8, K to Grade 3. | Summary: When Micah and his family volunteer to pick pumpkins for a soup kitchen, he also hopes to get the perfect pumpkin for himself, but soon learns that giving to others can be even better. Includes facts about Sukkot.
Identifiers: LCCN 2016028084 | ISBN 9781512408638 (lb : alk. paper) | ISBN 9781512408652 (pb : alk. paper)
Subjects: | CYAC: Generosity—Fiction. | Pumpkin—Fiction. | Sukkot—Fiction. | Jews–United States–Fiction.
Classification: LCC PZ7.1.S74334 Bes 2017 | DDC [E]—dc23

LC record available at https://lccn.loc.gov/2016028084

Manufactured in China
1-39490-21224-3/14/2017

091723.1K1/B1086/A5

The Best SUKKOT PUMPKIN EVER

Laya Steinberg

Illustrations by
Colleen Madden

KAR-BEN
PUBLISHING

Micah leaped out of the car, landing in tractor tracks that snaked through the mud by the edge of a huge field. "I'm going to find the best pumpkin ever!" he exclaimed.

A cool breeze mussed up Micah's hair. "This chilly fall wind is chasing away the last bit of summer," said Mom.

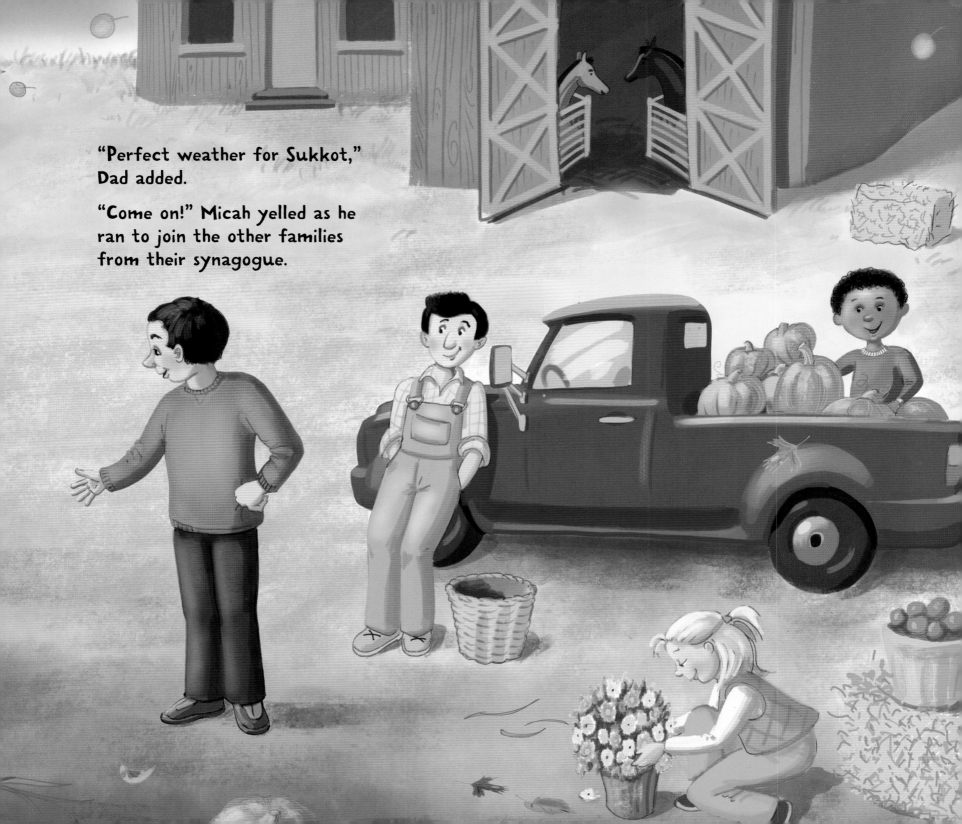

"Perfect weather for Sukkot," Dad added.

"Come on!" Micah yelled as he ran to join the other families from their synagogue.

"Thanks for volunteering," said Farmer Jared. "We have lots of pumpkins to pick before the frost comes. The more you find, the more we'll donate to the soup kitchen."

"What's a soup kitchen?" Micah whispered to his mother.

"**A** place where **people** in **need** can go to get a **meal** without having to **pay** for it," **Mom** replied.

Farmer Jared nodded. "Our pumpkins will feed lots of hungry people."

Dad explained, "When we help others like that, we're taking part in *tikkun olam*, repairing the world."

"And in return for helping out, each of you can choose a pumpkin to take home," Farmer Jared added.

"I'm going to save my pumpkin for Sukkot!" Micah said.

The children raced into the field. Some pumpkins were
easy to spot, their skins glowing like the midday sun,
but Micah was on the lookout for a great big one.

Micah got down on his hands and knees and lifted a giant leaf. "Ouch!" The vine was prickly. But underneath was a perfectly ripe pumpkin.

"Found one!"

He yanked and pulled, wrenched and twisted, until finally it came free from the vine. Micah pushed aside more leaves. "And another!"

Micah collected more and more pumpkins—some with smooth skins, some with ridges, and even a lumpy one that was flat on one side. But not one was big enough to be his perfect Sukkot pumpkin.

"Look at how many we picked!" Lila exclaimed.

"But I still haven't found the best one," said Micah.

Micah ran to the farthest corner of the field. He searched and foraged, lifted and shifted, until finally . . .

"I found it!" Micah yelled. He threw his arms around a huge pumpkin, as round and full as the moon on Sukkot.

Micah heaved and tugged, pushed and shoved. The pumpkin wouldn't budge. "I need help!" Micah called out. Other kids came running.

"This must weigh more than a tractor!" Ari exclaimed when he tried to lift the pumpkin.

Together they rolled the pumpkin all the way back to the truck.

Micah couldn't wait to show off his enormous, perfect pumpkin.

Then Micah remembered what Farmer Jared had said about the soup kitchen.

Micah took a deep breath and said to Farmer Jared, "Here. This one's for soup."

Farmer Jared smiled. "What a kind offer! We don't use the large pumpkins for cooking, but it will make a wonderful decoration."

Micah headed back to the field.

He searched and scoured, raked and rummaged. Finally he spotted it—a perfect little **pumpkin**, the best Sukkot **pumpkin** ever.

Micah could almost taste the delicious soup and the sweet and spicy pumpkin pie this pumpkin would make. His family always had so much delicious food on Sukkot.

Not everyone was as lucky as his family.

Micah placed his perfect small pumpkin on Farmer Jared's truck. "This one is for the soup kitchen, too—for cooking," he said proudly.

As he stepped back, he felt something squishy beneath his feet. It was a spongy, moldy pumpkin, and it smelled like wet socks. "Eww! This one's rotten!"

"That pumpkin will break down into compost and feed the soil next spring," Farmer Jared explained.

Micah knelt down. He pried open the pumpkin's mushy flesh and studied the inside. It was filled with seeds.

He scooped out a few and slipped them into his pocket.

Micah rushed over to his mom. "Look, Mom!" He held out his empty hands. "I found the best pumpkin!"

"Is your pumpkin invisible?" asked Mom.

Micah laughed. "I donated my perfect big pumpkin to be a decoration. I donated my perfect small one for soup. And I left the perfectly mushy one for compost! But I kept these." Micah smiled as he pulled out his seeds.

"The best Sukkot pumpkins ever—
for next year."

ABOUT SUKKOT

Sukkot, which means "huts," is the Jewish harvest holiday that commemorates the forty years the Israelites wandered in the desert and lived in temporary shelters.

Many families build and decorate their own sukkah, and eat their meals in the sukkah. Some even sleep in their sukkah! A sukkah has at least three sides, plus a roof made of *schach*—branches or large leaves or cornstalks. The roof provides shade from the sun but also allows the stars to be seen at night.

TIKKUN OLAM ACTIVITIES FOR FAMILIES:

Volunteer to serve food at a soup kitchen or homeless shelter.

Plant a garden and donate the vegetables to a food shelf.

Collect blankets and towels for a homeless shelter or refugee aid center.

Collect recyclable cans and bottles, take them to a store or center that pays a small amount of money for them, and donate the money to charity.

Donate stuffed animals to the local police or fire department to comfort children in crisis situations.

LAYA STEINBERG is the author of two award-winning picture books. When she's not writing for young people, she's teaching art and design to high school students, tending a donation garden, or in her basement pottery studio making crazy-shaped bowls and plates. She lives near Boston, Massachusetts with her husband, kids and various-sized furry critters who squeak when she comes home with vegetables.

COLLEEN MADDEN is an illustrator of many children's books. When she's not drawing and daydreaming, she's out chasing chipmunks on a trail, learning how to make socks, and eating lots and lots of sushi! She works and lives in the Philadelphia area.